Enid Blyton

A WISHING-CHAIR
ADVENTURE

THE ROYAL
BIRTHDAY PARTY

For Hamish
A. P.

EGMONT
We bring stories to life

Cover and interior illustrations by Alex Paterson

Text published as chapter 4 of *More Wishing-Chair Stories* 2000
and chapter 11 of *The Adventures of the Wishing-Chair* 1937
Published as *The Royal Birthday: A Wishing-Chair Adventure* 2019
by Egmont UK Limited
The Yellow Building, 1 Nicholas Road, London W11 4AN

Enid Blyton ® and Enid Blyton's signature are registered
trade marks of Hodder & Stoughton Limited
Text copyright © Hodder & Stoughton Limited
Illustrations copyright © Hodder & Stoughton Limited

ISBN 978 1 4052 9266 5

www.egmont.co.uk

A CIP catalogue record for this title is available from the British Library

Printed in Malaysia

68895/001

Stay safe online. Any website addresses listed in this book are correct
at the time of going to print. However, Egmont is not responsible
for content hosted by third parties. Please be aware that online content
can be subject to change and websites can contain content
that is unsuitable for children. We advise that all children are
supervised when using the internet.

Egmont takes its responsibility to the planet and its inhabitants very seriously.
We aim to use papers from well-managed forests run by responsible suppliers.

Enid Blyton

A WISHING-CHAIR
ADVENTURE

THE ROYAL
BIRTHDAY PARTY

EGMONT

CHAPTER ONE
LAND OF WISHES

The chair was a bit crowded, with the two children, Nose-About the brownie, and Binky.

'I'll take you to the **Land of Wishes** if you like,' said the small brownie, humbly. He was very anxious to please them all. 'You can have as many wishes as you like this weekend because it's **Princess Peronel's birthday**. I've an invitation ticket. Look.'

He pulled a rather crumpled ticket from his pocket. It certainly was an **invitation**.

'But it's for you, not for us,' said Peter.

'It says "For Brownie Nose-About *and Friends*",' said the brownie. 'I'm Nose-About – and **you're my friends**, aren't you? Oh, please do say you are!'

'Well – all right, we're your friends then,' said Peter.

'Mollie certainly *was* a friend to you in **the Village of Gobbo!** Binky, shall we go to the Land of Wishes? I know quite a few wishes I'd like to wish!'

'Yes, let's go,' said Binky. 'Nose-About, *you'd* better tell the chair to go, because you're the one who has the invitation.'

So, in a rather important voice, Nose-About told the chair where to go. 'To the Land of Wishes, please,' he said. 'To the Princess Peronel's birthday party.'

The chair gave a little creak and flew straight upwards. It was very dark now and **stars were out in the sky**.

Mollie began to feel **sleepy**. She nodded her head and leant against Peter. Peter nodded his head, too, and both of them slept soundly. Binky and Nose-About kept

guard. The chair flew all night long, for the Land of Wishes was a **long, long way away**.

8

CHAPTER TWO
A PRINCE AND PRINCESS

The sun was up and the sky was full of light when at last the two children awoke. Below them was a land of flowers and lakes and streams and **shining palaces**. How lovely!

'Does *everyone* live in a palace here?' asked Mollie, marvelling at so many palaces.

'Oh, yes. It's easy enough to wish for one,' said Nose-About, peering down. 'And then when you're tired of living in an enormous place with windows everywhere, you just wish for a **rose-covered cottage**. Would you like a palace for a bit? I'll wish you one!'

The chair flew downwards. It landed in a field of shining, star-like flowers. 'Here we are,' said the brownie. 'I'll wish for a palace to begin with – and then we can be **princes and a princess**, and go to Princess Peronel's birthday party.

I wish for a palace with one thousand and one windows!' And **silently and shimmeringly** a tall, slender palace rose up round them. The sun shone in through hundreds of windows.

'I'll just count if there *are* a thousand and one,' said Nose-About.

'Oh *no*! We simply *can't* count up to a thousand and one all over again!' groaned Peter. 'I say – look at the wishing-chair. It's standing on that platform there wishing it was a **throne!**'

'I wish it *was* a throne!' said Mollie at once. And dear me, the good old wishing-chair changed into a gleaming throne, with a big red velvet cushion on its seat and tassels hanging down its back. It looked **very grand indeed**.

Peter went and sat on it. 'I wish I was a prince!' he said. And to Mollie's enormous surprise her brother suddenly looked like a very **handsome little prince**, with a circlet of gold round his head and a beautiful cloak hanging from his velvet-clad shoulders. He grinned at Mollie. 'Better wish yourself to be a princess before I order you about!' he said. 'I feel like giving a whole lot of orders! Where's my horse? Where are my dogs? **Where are my servants?**'

Well, before very long Mollie was a princess, and looked quite beautiful in a dress that swept the ground and twinkled with **thousands of bright jewels** as she walked. Binky wished himself a new suit and a new wand. Nose-About still felt very humble so he didn't wish for anything for himself but only things for the others.

He wished for horses and dogs and
cats and servants and **ice-creams** and
everything he could think of.

'I think we've got enough dogs, Nose-
About,' said Peter at last. 'And I'd rather
not have any more ice-creams. I feel
rather as if I'd like **a good breakfast**.
All the clocks you wished for have just
struck nine o'clock. I feel hungry.'

The brownie wished for so much
porridge and bacon and eggs that
there was enough for the cats and dogs too.
The servants had taken the horses out of
the palace, which made Mollie feel more
comfortable, because when the brownie
had first wished for them they kept
galloping round the enormous room.
She was afraid of being knocked over.

That was a most exciting morning. When the children got into the way of wishing there was no end to the things they thought of!

'**I feel like snowballing!** I wish for plenty of snow!' said Peter, suddenly. And outside the palace windows fell the snowflakes, thick and fast. There was soon enough for a **game**.

It was very easy to wish the snow away when they were tired of snowballing and wish for something else – an **aeroplane** they could fly, or a train they could drive.

'I wish this would last all over our weekend,' sighed Mollie. **'I'm enjoying it so.'**

'Well – I suppose it will,' said Peter, 'Now you've wished it, **the wish will come true**. But what about Mother? She won't like it if we stay away all the time.'

'I'll wish *her* here, then,' said Mollie. But Peter wouldn't let her.

'No. Don't,' he said. 'If she's with Granny she wouldn't like leaving her – and it would upset Granny to see Mother suddenly disappear. We'll just enjoy ourselves here, and then try and explain to Mother when we get home.'

CHAPTER THREE
THE ROYAL PARTY

The princess's party was wonderful. It began at four o'clock that afternoon, and lasted till past midnight. There was a **birthday cake** that was so very big it took six little servants to cut it into slices. One hundred candles burnt on it! How old Peronel must be!

'A hundred years old is *young* for a fairy,' said Binky. 'See how **beautiful** the princess still is.'

She certainly was. Peter wished hard for a dance with her – and at once she **glided** over to him, and danced as lightly as a moth. 'Now I can say I've danced with a princess!' thought Peter, pleased.

The next day came and slid away
happily. Then the next day and the next.
The children grew used to having every
single wish granted.

'A **big chocolate ice** at once!' And hey presto, it came.

'A **tame lion** to ride on!' There it was, purring like a cat.

'Wings on my back to fly high above
the trees!' And there they were, **fluttering
strongly**, carrying Mollie high in the air.
What a truly lovely feeling.

On that fourth day the children didn't wish quite so many things. **'Tired of wishing?'** asked Binky, who hadn't really wished many things. 'Ah – people always get tired of wishes coming true after a time.'

'I can't seem to think of any more,' said
Peter.

'*I* keep thinking of Mother,' said Mollie.
'I do so hope she isn't worried about us.
We've got to go back home today, Peter
– do you realise that? It's the day we have
to go **back to school**. It's a pity we've
had so little time at home. We shall hardly
have seen Daddy and Mother at all.'

'Oh goodness – how the weekend has
flown,' said Peter. 'I wanted to do quite a
lot of things at home, too. I wanted to get
out **my electric train** – and didn't you
want to take your dolls out just once in
their pram, Mollie?'

'Yes, I did,' said Mollie. 'Oh dear – I do
wish we had the weekend in front of us
still, so that we could enjoy being at home,

too! I feel as if we've rather wasted it now. Peter, I think we ought to go back. We've a train to catch, you know. We mustn't be late back for school.'

'All right. Binky, we'd better change the throne back to the wishing-chair,' said Peter. '**Wish for its wings, will you?** They've gone, but a wish will bring them back, in the Land of Wishes!'

CHAPTER FOUR
BACK TO SCHOOL

It did, of course. As soon as the throne had
changed back into the wishing-chair they
knew so well, Binky wished for the wings
to grow – and they sprouted out gaily, at
once, looking **bigger** than ever.

'You coming, Nose-About?' said Peter to
the little brownie.

'No. I'm going back home to my
mother,' he said. 'Goodbye. Thank you for
being kind to me.'

'Well, you've certainly repaid our
kindness!' said Mollie. 'I've never had
such a wonderful time in my life. Now –

are we all ready? Wishing-chair, home, please, as fast as you can!'

It was a **long, long way** back from the Land of Wishes. They all three went sound asleep, and the chair was careful not to jolt them at all in case they fell off. It flew down to the playroom at last, and went in gently at the door. It tipped out Mollie and Peter on to their mattresses, and Binky on to his cushion.

The children groaned a little, and then **slept on soundly**, curled up on their mattresses. The chair stood still. Its red wings disappeared gradually. It was just a chair.

And then there came a loud knocking at the door, and a loud voice, too.

'Peter! Mollie! How late you are sleeping! Haven't you had your **breakfast** yet? Your mother has telephoned to say that Granny is much better and she'll be home to lunch. Isn't that good news?'

The children woke up with a **jump** and stared at Mrs Williams' smiling face. She was looking in at the door. Peter sat up and rubbed his eyes. 'Well, I declare!' said Mrs Williams. 'You are not in your night-things! You don't mean to say you didn't go to bed properly last night? Do wake up. It's half-past ten already!'

'Half-past ten?' said Mollie, amazed. 'What day is it, Mrs Williams?'

'**Saturday, to be sure!**' said Mrs Williams, surprised. 'You came home yesterday, that was Friday – and so today's Saturday!'

'But – but surely it's Tuesday or perhaps even Wednesday,' said Mollie, remembering the wonderful weekend in the Land of Wishes. 'Aren't we due back at school?'

'Bless us all, you're asleep and dreaming!' said Mrs Williams. 'Well, I must be getting on with my work. It's Saturday morning, half-past ten, and your mother will be home for lunch. Now – do you understand *that*?'

And off she went, quite **puzzled**. She hadn't seen Binky on the cushion. He was still fast asleep!

Mollie looked at Peter and her eyes shone. 'Peter, oh Peter!' she said, 'do you remember that I wished we had the weekend in front of us still? Well, that wish has come true, too. We've *had* the weekend once in our palace – and now we're going to have it all over again at home. **Could anything be nicer!**'

'Marvellous!' said Peter, jumping up.

'Simply marvellous! Wake up, you lazy old Binky. We've good news for you. It's not Tuesday – it's only Saturday!'

So there they are, just going to welcome their mother back again, and looking forward to **a wonderful half-term.** 'Crreee-eee-eak!' says the good old wishing-chair, happily.

CHAPTER FIVE
THE MAGICIAN'S PARTY

One afternoon, when the children and
Binky were **reading stories**, there came a
timid knock at the door. 'Come in!' called
Mollie. The door opened and in came two
small elves. 'May we speak to Binky?' they
asked. Binky waved them to a chair.

'Sit down,' he said. 'What do you want?'

'Please, may we borrow your wishing-chair to go to the **Magician Greatheart's party**,' said the bigger elf.

'Well, it doesn't belong to me,' said Binky. 'It belongs to these two children.'

'Would you let us borrow it?' asked the little elves.

'Certainly,' said Mollie and Peter.

'What reward do you ask?' said the elves.

'Oh, you can have the chair for nothing,' said Mollie. 'Bring it back safely, that's all.'

'I suppose you wouldn't like to come to the party?' asked the elves. 'We are very **small**, and there are only five of us to go. There would be plenty of room for you and for Binky too in the chair.'

'**Stars and moon**, what a treat!' cried Binky in delight. 'Yes, we'll all go! Thanks very much! Greatheart's parties are glorious! My word, this *is* luck! When is the party, elves?'

'Tomorrow night,' said the elves. 'Sharp at midnight.

We'll be here at half-past eleven.'

'Right,' said Binky. The little elves said good-bye and ran out. Binky rubbed his hands and turned to the two delighted children.

'The **magician** is a marvellous fellow,' he said. 'He is a good magician, and the enchantments and magic he knows are perfectly wonderful. I hope he does a few tricks! Put on your best clothes and be here at half-past eleven tomorrow night, won't you!'

The children were most excited. They talked about nothing else all day long and the next day too. They dressed themselves in their **best clothes** and

ran down to the playroom at half-past
eleven the next night. Binky was there too,
looking very grand indeed, for he had on
a suit that seemed to be made of **silver
moonbeams** sewn with pearls.

The elves were there waiting, all dressed daintily in flower petals, sewn with spider thread. Even the wishing-chair looked smart, for Binky had tied **a big bow** on each of its arms! Its red wings were lazily flapping.

The children got in and Binky sat on the back. The five little elves easily found room on the two arms. Off they went, flying through the **moonlight** to their great and wonderful party!

CHAPTER SIX
A VERY MAGICAL PALACE

The magician's **palace** was set on top of a high hill. The chair did not take long to get there. It flew down and took its place among the long line of **carriages** that were drawing up one by one at the big front door.

When their turn came the children
and the elves jumped off the chair and
ran up the steps. They were shown into
a great hall and there they shook hands
with Magician Greatheart, a tall and
handsome enchanter, whose cloak rippled
out as he walked, as if it were made of
blue water. His eyes were kind and
looked right through
everyone.

A band was playing merrily in the big
hall, and Binky caught hold of Mollie and
danced with her. Peter found a small, shy
fairy and danced with her too, though she
was so light that he couldn't make up his
mind if she was real or not!

There were hundreds of **fairy folk** there of all kinds – gnomes, goblins, brownies, fairies, elves, pixies – but only two children, so Mollie and Peter felt most honoured.

Then came the supper. It was so queer. The long, long table was spread with plates and glasses and dishes, but there was no food at all, no, not even a **yellow jelly**.

The magician took his place at the end of the table. 'Will you each wish for what you like **best to eat?**' he said in his kind, deep voice. 'Take it in turn, please!'

A brownie next to him said, 'I wish for **honey-lemonade** and sugar biscuits!'

At once a jug of yellow lemonade appeared by him and a plate of delicious sugar biscuits! The fairy next to the brownie wished for chocolate blancmange and a cream ice. They appeared even as she spoke the words! It was such fun to see them come.

Mollie and Peter watched in **amazement** as all the dishes and jugs on the table became full of the most exciting

things when each little creature wished his or her wish. They had their turns too!

'I wish for cream buns and ginger-beer!' said Mollie.

'And I wish for treacle pudding and lemonade!' said Peter. A dish of **cream buns** and a bottle of fizzy ginger-beer appeared in front of Mollie, and a dish with a **steaming hot treacle pudding** and a jug of lemonade appeared by Peter. It was just like a dream!

Everyone ate and drank and was **merry** as could be. Then, after the supper, the magician spoke one strange word, and the long, long table, with its dishes and plates, vanished into thin air!

'Now we will have some **magic!**' said the magician, beaming at his excited guests.

CHAPTER SEVEN
WAS IT ALL A DREAM

They all sat down on the floor. The magician took a silver stick and tapped three times on the floor. A spire of **green smoke** came up and made a crackling noise. It shot up into the air, turned over and over and wound its way among the guests, dropping tiny bunches of sweet-smelling flowers as it passed – **buttonholes** for every one!

The **smoke** went. The magician tapped the floor again and up rose five black cats, each with a violin except the last one, and he had a **drum**.

After the cats came six plump **rabbits**, who danced to the tunes that the cats played. One rabbit turned upside down and danced on his ears, and that made Peter laugh so much that he had to get out his handkerchief to wipe his tears of **laughter** away.

Then an even stranger thing happened next. The magician tapped the floor once more, and up came a great flower of yellow. It opened, and in the middle of it the guests could see **five red eggs**.

The eggs broke and out came tiny
chicks. They grew – and grew – and grew
– and became great **brilliant birds** with
long drooping tails. Then they opened
their beaks and sang so sweetly that not a
sound could be heard in the great hall but
their voices.

The birds flew away. The flower faded. The magician tapped the floor for the last time. A **gnome** appeared, whose long beard floated round him like a mist. He handed Greatheart a big dish with a lid. The magician took off the lid and lifted out a **silver spoon**. He stirred in the air and a bubbling sound came. Round the spoon grew a glass bowl.

The children could see the spoon shining in it. But suddenly the spoon turned to gold and swam about – a **live goldfish**.

Greatheart took the goldfish neatly
into his hand and threw it into the air. It
disappeared.

'Who has it?' asked Greatheart.

Everyone looked about – but no one had
the fish. Greatheart **laughed** and went
over to Mollie. He put his hand into her
right ear and pulled out the goldfish!

Then he took up Peter's hand and opened it — and will you believe it, Peter had a **little yellow chick** there, cheeping away merrily!

Oh, the tricks that the magician did! No one would ever believe them! Peter and Mollie rubbed their eyes several times and wondered if they were **dreaming**.

Best of all came the last trick. The magician, as he said good-night to his guests, gave each a tiny egg.

'It will hatch tomorrow,' he said. 'Keep it safely!' The children thanked him very much for a marvellous evening, and then got sleepily into the wishing-chair with Binky and the elves. How they got home they never knew — for there must have been **magic** about that took them home, undressed them, and popped them into bed without their knowing. Anyway, they found themselves there the next morning when they awoke, although they did not remember at all how they got there!

'I believe it was all a **beautiful dream**,' said Mollie.

'It wasn't!' said Peter, putting his hand under his pillow. He brought out his little egg. As he looked at it, it broke – and there, in his hand, was a **tiny silver watch**, ticking away merrily!

Mollie gave a scream of delight and put her hand under her pillow to get her egg too. It broke in her hand – and out of it came a necklace of beads that looked exactly like **bubbles!** It was the loveliest one Mollie had ever seen!

'Hurry up and dress and we'll see what Binky got,' said Mollie. They hurried – and when they saw Binky, he showed them *his* present – **golden buckles** for his shoes. Didn't they look grand!

'That was the loveliest party I've ever been to!' said Mollie happily. 'I wish *all* our wishing-chair adventures were like that!'

The FARAWAY TREE Adventure

Collect them All!

Enid Blyton
A FARAWAY TREE Adventure

The Land of
BIRTHDAYS

Enid Blyton
A FARAWAY TREE Adventure

The Land of MAGIC
MEDICINES

Enid Blyton
A FARAWAY TREE Adventure

The Land of
DO-AS-YOU-PLEASE

Enid Blyton
A FARAWAY TREE Adventure

The Land of
GOODIES

Enid Blyton
A FARAWAY TREE Adventure

In SANTA
CLAUS'S CASTLE

Enid Blyton
A FARAWAY TREE Adventure

The Land of
TOYS

Enid Blyton
A FARAWAY TREE Adventure

The Land of
DREAMS

Enid Blyton
A FARAWAY TREE Adventure

The Land of
ENCHANTMENTS

Enid Blyton
A FARAWAY TREE Adventure

The Land of
SILLY SCHOOL

Enid Blyton
A FARAWAY TREE Adventure

JOE and the
MAGIC SNOWMAN

Classic short stories from the
magical Faraway Tree series – packed
full of exciting new colour illustrations